My travelin' eye →

A Note from the Author

"Travelin' eye," or strabismus, is when one eye, or both eyes,
misaligns and turns in, out, up, or down.
Lazy eye, or amblyopia, is reduced vision, when the brain
does not fully acknowledge the images seen by the eye.
Jenny Sue has both.

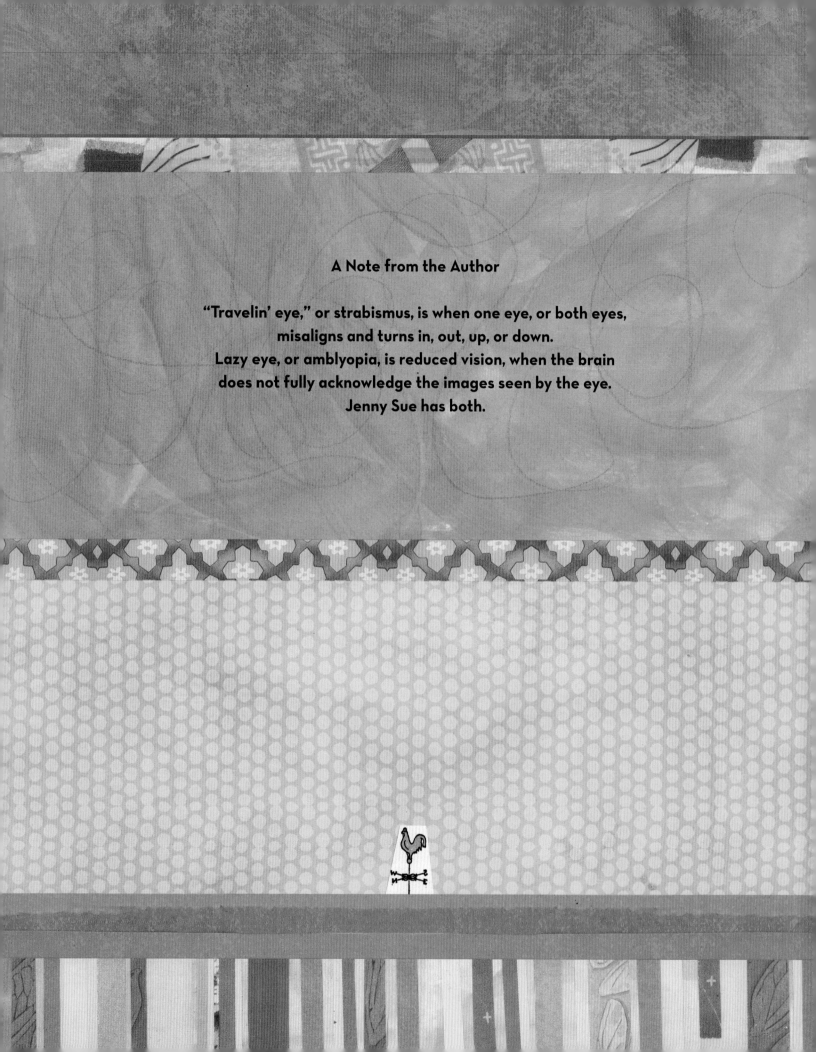

For God.

And for Mom and Dad
(my biggest cheerleaders).
Thank you
for believing in me.
I love you!

Henry Holt and Company, LLC, *Publishers since 1866*
175 Fifth Avenue, New York, New York 10010
www.HenryHoltKids.com

Henry Holt® is a registered trademark of Henry Holt and Company, LLC.
Copyright © 2008 by Jenny Sue Kostecki-Shaw
All rights reserved.
Distributed in Canada by H. B. Fenn and Company Ltd.

Library of Congress Cataloging-in-Publication Data
Kostecki-Shaw, Jenny Sue.
My travelin' eye / Jenny Sue Kostecki-Shaw.—1st ed.
p.   cm.
Summary: Jenny Sue loves that her "travelin' eye" lets her see the world in
a special way, and so she is not happy when her teacher suggests that her
parents take her to an ophthalmologist to fix the lazy eye.
ISBN-13: 978-0-8050-8169-5 / ISBN-10: 0-8050-8169-0
[1. Eye—Fiction. 2. Vision—Fiction. 3. Individuality—Fiction. 4. Schools—
Fiction.] I. Title. II. Title: My traveling eye.
PZ7.K85278My 2008   [E]—dc22   2007007224

First Edition—2008 / Designed by Amelia May Anderson
The artist used acrylics, crayon, pencil, collage, and tissue paper on
Strathmore illustration board to create the illustrations for this book.
Printed in China on acid-free paper. ∞

10 9 8 7 6 5 4 3 2 1

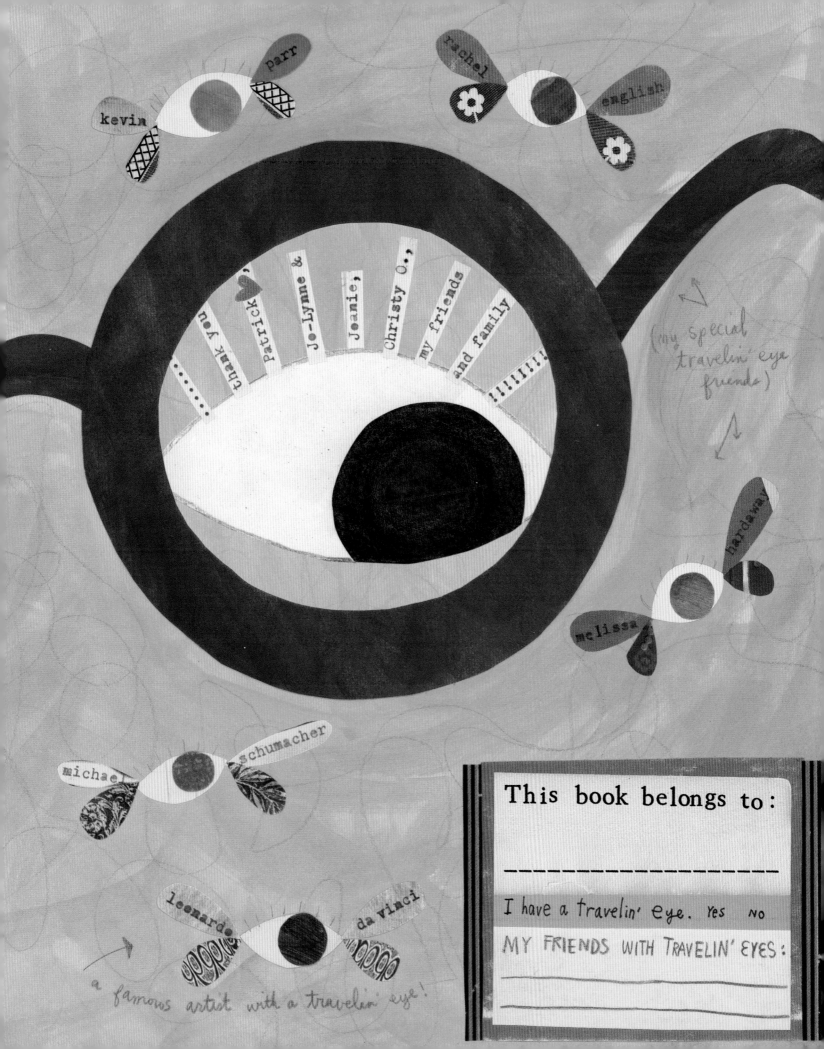

kevin parr

rachel english

thank you Patrick ♥, Jo-Lynne & Joanie, Christy O., my friends and family !!!!!!!!

(my special travelin' eye friends)

hardaway

melissa

michael schumacher

leonardo da vinci

→ a famous artist with a travelin' eye!

This book belongs to:

_____

I have a travelin' eye. Yes   No

MY FRIENDS WITH TRAVELIN' EYES:

_____

_____

When I was born, I came out looking both ways.

I remember hearing someone whisper,
"She's got a wandering eye!"

But I prefer

to call it a "travelin' eye,"

because everywhere it goes . . .

I follow.

Sometimes kids make fun of me because
I am looking in two directions at the same time.
They say I have "iguana eyes."

I guess they're right.

But
I think
**iguanas
are cool,**
so
I must
be,
too.

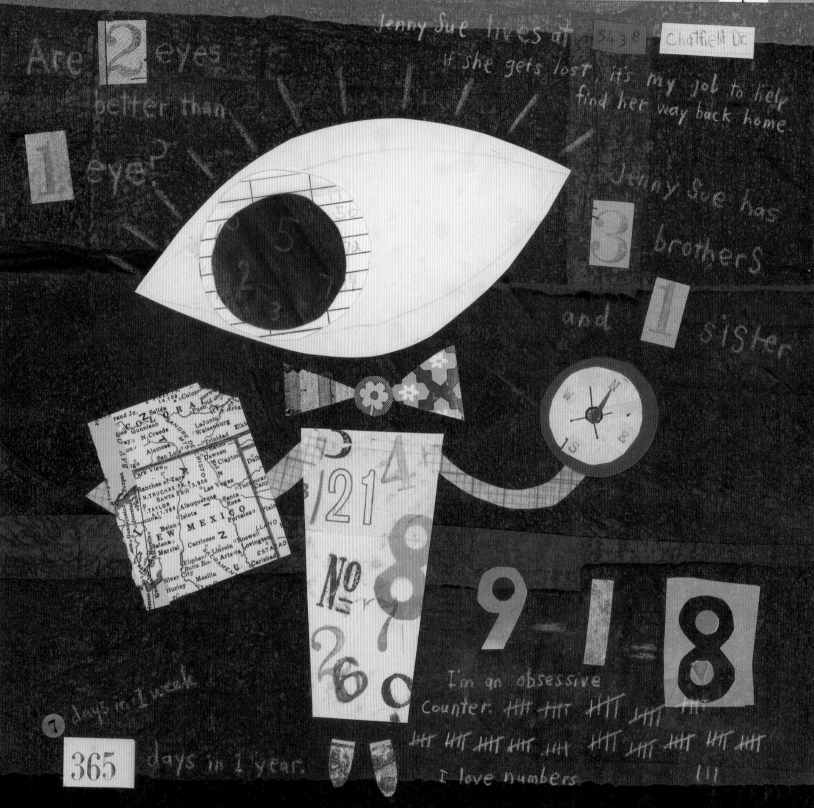

My right eye is the navigator.

It sees numbers. It's my guide.

red + yellow = orange

Chasing rainbows is my expertise.

self portrait

A GREAT team

My travelin' eye is the artist. It sees colors.

It's the adventurer. Together, we make a great team.

My travelin' eye reminds me to look **around.**

And up and down.

To smell the flowers, kiss the butterflies,
and read the clouds.

But other times its wandering nature gets me into trouble.

One day, my teacher sent a note home
suggesting I see an ophthalmologist to "fix"
my eye so it wouldn't stare out the window.

"No thank you,"

I said to my mom and dad.

"My
eye
isn't
broken."

(Plus,
I was
scared
to see
an
ophthalmologist.)

EYE
DOCTOR

Ring
Bell

BABY

But Mom took me anyway.

The
ophthalmologist's
name
was
Dr. Dave,
and he was quite ordinary looking—to my relief.

He asked me to follow his finger around the room with my eyes.

Simple, I thought.

He began tracing a big circle with his long index finger. My right eye followed his finger to the left, but my travelin' eye went right. My right eye followed his finger up, but my travelin' eye went down.

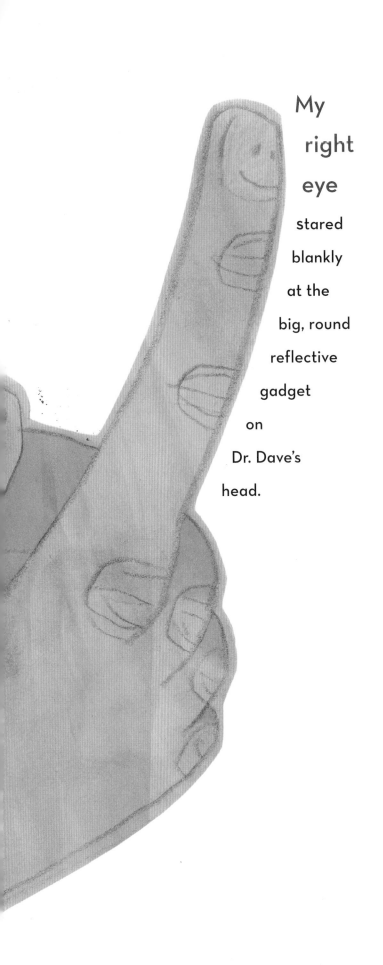

My
right
eye
stared
blankly
at the
big, round
reflective
gadget
on
Dr. Dave's
head.

My
travelin'
eye
was
busy
looking
at
everything
else.

He stuck a plain round patch over my right eye.
He said that should "strengthen the lazy one."

He
also
gave
me
glasses—

BIG,

thick

red

ones.

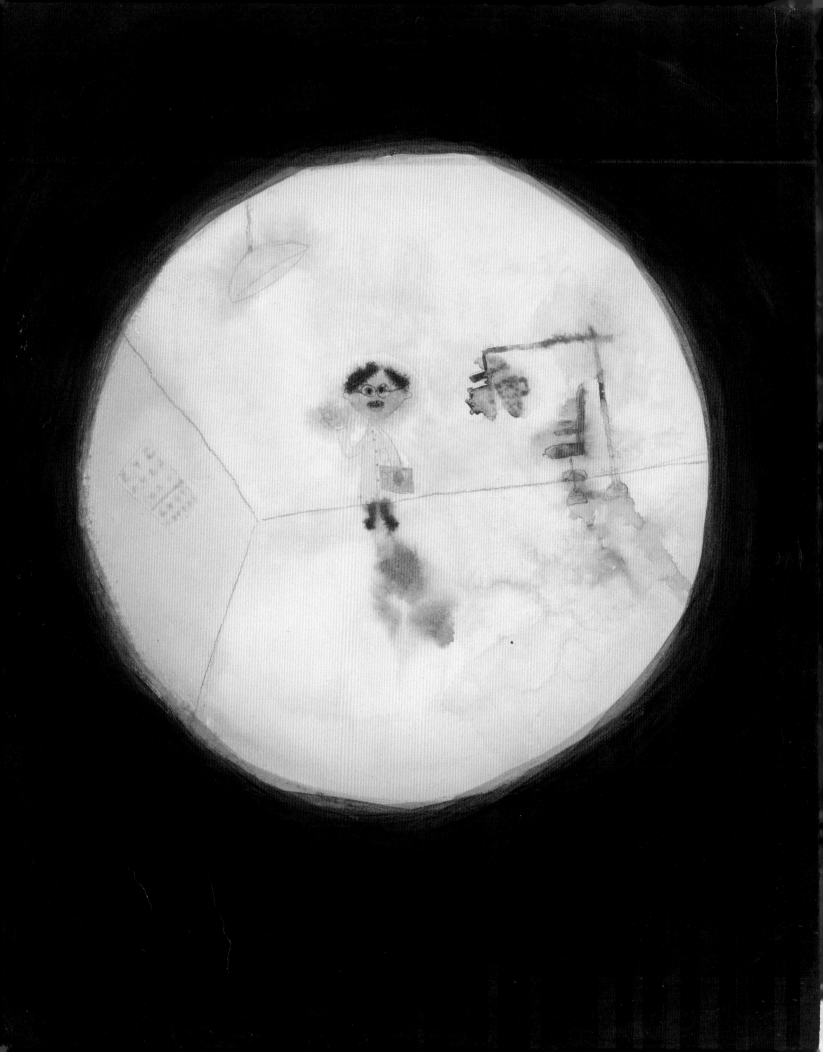

Everything became mostly black and confusing.

Dr.

Dave

looked

so

small

and

so

far

away.

At school,
kids pointed.

Letters floated around the chalkboard,
and I couldn't make sense of them.

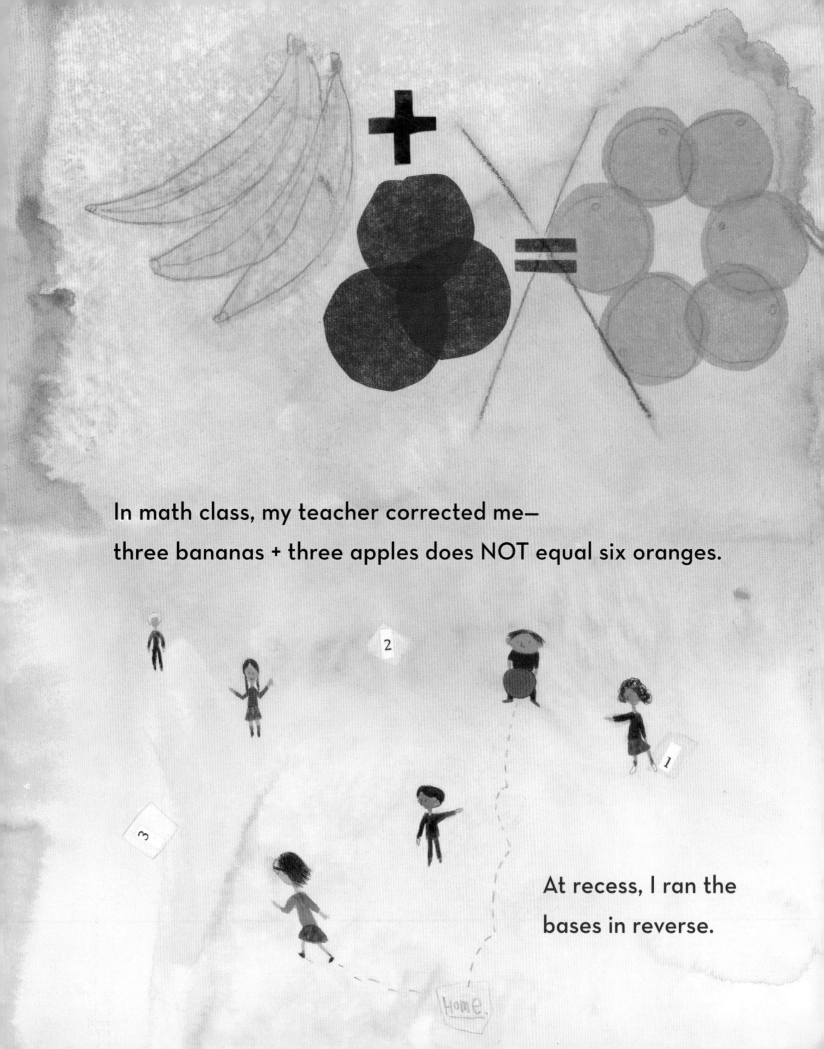

In math class, my teacher corrected me—
three bananas + three apples does NOT equal six oranges.

At recess, I ran the
bases in reverse.

On
the way
home
from
school,
**I thought
I saw
an
elephant
sitting
in a
tree.**

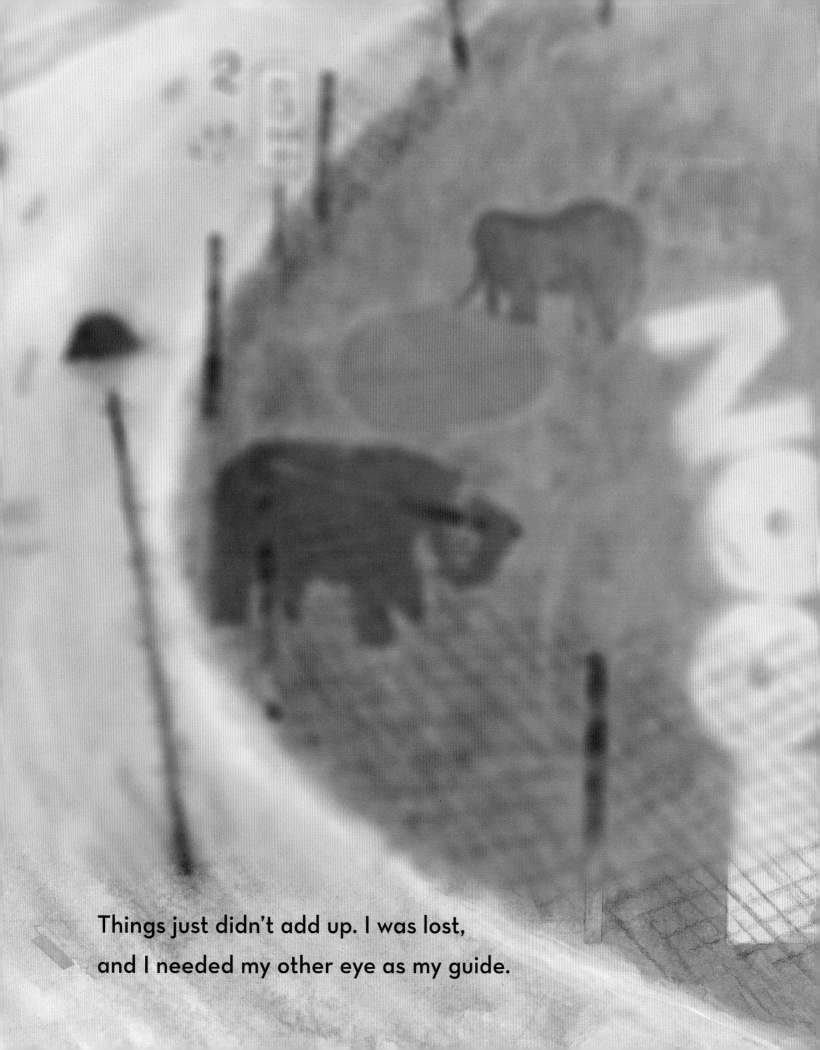

Things just didn't add up. I was lost,
and I needed my other eye as my guide.

That night I cried myself to sleep

and dreamed I sailed

far ___ away

from everything that made me sad.

3 Eyes!

The next morning, I told my mom how sad I felt.
I told her I didn't ever want to go back to school.

"Hmmm," she thought out loud. "Jenny Sue,
I think we just have to get creative!"

And with
Mom's help,
I made
my first
"fashion-patch."

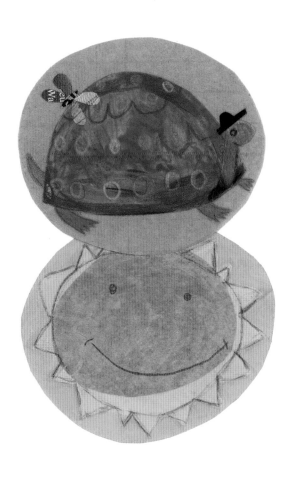

Soon, all the kids at school wanted to wear a "fashion-patch," but they couldn't, not without a note from their ophthalmologist.

Little by little, my world came into focus,

and I made a new fashion-patch every day.

My travelin' eye was far from being a lazy eye!

It was busy noticing all sorts of things.

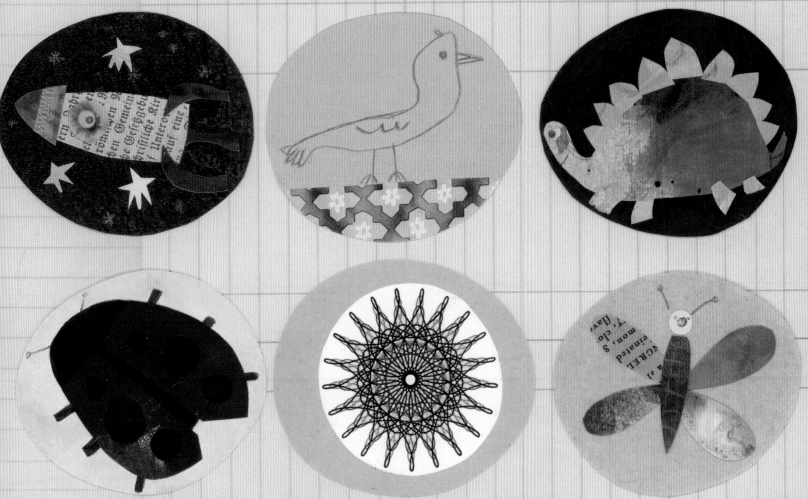

Before I knew it, it was time to go back to see Dr. Dave.

"Well, Jenny Sue, how are you?"

Dr. Dave
asked,
staring
straight
into
my
lone
eye.

He instructed me to follow his finger with my travelin' eye. It slowly followed.

Then he peeled off my butterfly patch. It took a minute for my right eye to adjust to the light after being in the dark for so long. He asked me to follow his finger again, this time with both eyes. **The real test.**

I closed
my eyes
and
took
a deep
breath.
When
I opened
them,
I followed
Dr. Dave's
finger
as it
floated
around
in a
giant circle

. . . to the left . . . up and over to the right . . . down . . . and back to center. I held my breath waiting to hear if I passed.

It has woken up!"

My travelin' eye had grown stronger. And more confident. I think it just needed some special attention. My one-eyed days were over!

It was awake all along.

But the glasses— they were here to stay. And that was okay, because they did help me see everything better.

Together, Mom and I fashioned up my new glasses.
Of course, all the kids at school wanted to wear fashion
glasses, but they couldn't, not without a special note
from their ophthalmologist.

My travelin' eye still wanders sometimes, but that's the true nature of an artist — to see the world in her own unique way.